中国经典故事

Chinese Classical Stories I

主 编／熊亮　　翻 译／范晓星

海豚出版社
DOLPHIN BOOKS

CIPG 中国国际出版集团

这套书就是一个小舞台，

让古老的故事活起来，

在纸上表演一出精彩的图画剧。

这就是我设计这套书的用意，

吸引孩子主动阅读下去。

熊亮（著名图画书作家）

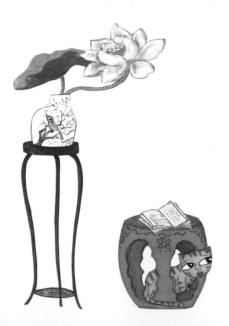

刻舟求剑

Marking a Boat to Recover a Sword

绘画/熊亮

改编/奇异堡

翻译/范晓星

从前，有个人坐船过江，不小心把剑掉到水里去了。

Once upon a time, a man was crossing a river in a ferry. He accidentally dropped his sword into the water.

他急忙在船舷上刻了个记号，说："我的剑就是从这儿掉下去的。"

The man immediately cut a mark on one side of the boat. "This is where my sword fell into the river."

他一直盯着这个记号。

He kept his eyes on the mark all along the way to shore.

船一靠岸，他就脱掉上衣。

As soon as the boat arrived at the dock, the man took off his clothes.

他从那个记号的位置跳到
水里去捞剑。

From where he made his mark,
he jumped into the river to look
for his sword.

他捞了半天，怎么也捞不到自己的剑，觉得非常奇怪。

Although he searched a long time, the man just could not find his sword. He felt very puzzled.

守株待兔

Waiting for Hares to Drop Dead

绘画/熊亮

改编/奇异堡

翻译/范晓星

古时候，有个农夫，在他的田里有个大树桩。

Once, there was a farmer. In his field there was a big tree stump.

一天，一只野兔追着蝴蝶玩，跑着跑着就冲到树桩这儿。

One day, a hare came hopping along, chasing a butterfly. It was hopping toward the stump.

"嘭"的一声，野兔撞在树桩上，死了。

"Ow!" The hare ran into the stump and broke its neck.

农夫发现了这只死兔子。

The farmer found the dead hare.

他一把拎起兔子,心想:"原来这里可以捡到兔子啊!"

He picked up the hare and thought, "Aha! This is the place to catch hares with no effort!"

这太轻松了！再也不用种田了。

This is so easy! So the farmer never worked in the fields again.

于是，他整天守在树桩旁，旁边的田地都荒了。

He stood waiting by the stump all day long, hoping for another hare.

可是，他再也没有捡到过兔子。

Yet he never came upon any dead hares there ever again.

高山流水
A Legendary Musical Friendship

绘画／熊亮
改编／奇异堡
翻译／范晓星

从前，有个著名的琴师叫伯牙，他琴艺高超。

There was once a famous *guqin* master named Bo Ya. He was an excellent musician.

一个夜晚，伯牙乘船游览。面对清风明月，他弹起琴来。

One moonlit night, Bo Ya was on a boat drifting slowly along a river. The cool breeze and bright moon inspired him to play his *guqin*.

琴声悠扬。"好！"忽听岸上有人喝彩。

Heavenly melodies wafted along the wind. "Bravo!" someone applauded from the bank.

伯牙一看，只见一个樵夫站在岸边。

Bo Ya looked, and saw a woodcutter standing on the riverside.

他立即请樵夫上船，
兴致勃勃地为他弹奏。

He invited the woodcutter aboard the boat. He happily played the *guqin* for him.

伯牙弹起赞美高山的曲调，樵夫说道："真好！我现在就像在高山的顶峰。"

Bo Ya played music in praise of the high mountains. The woodcutter exclaimed, "Magnificent! I feel like I'm standing on top of a mountain."

"群山巍峨雄伟，高耸入云，好像泰山一样。"

"A great mountain, high enough to cut through the clouds, like Mount Tai."

伯牙弹起赞美波涛的曲调，樵夫说道："真好！宽广浩荡，我好像看见了无边的大海。"

Bo Ya played music for the ocean. The woodcutter exclaimed, "Marvelous! How vast and mighty! I now feel like I'm gazing out at the boundless sea."

伯牙激动地说："知音！你真是我的知音！"这个樵夫就是钟子期。

Bo Ya said excitedly, "A perfect friend! You truly understand my music!"

This woodcutter was the legendary Zhong Ziqi.

木兰从军

The Legend of Hua Mulan

绘画/彭婷

改编/奇异堡

翻译/范晓星

古时候，有个叫木兰的姑娘，从小喜欢骑马舞剑。

In ancient China, there lived a girl named Mulan. She was a girl who liked to ride horses and do martial arts.

一天，官府来村里征兵。木兰父亲的名字和其他年轻人一样出现在名册里。

One day, the imperial army came to recruit soldiers in her village. Mulan's father was on their list of names.

父亲年老多病，木兰请求替
父从军。

Mulan's father was very old and
sick. Mulan decided to join the
army in her father's place.

她剪短了长发，女扮男装。

She cut off her long hair, and disguised herself as a young man.

木兰在集市上买来骏马
配好马鞍, 替父亲出征。

Mulan bought a horse and saddled
at the market, and was ready to set off
in her father's place.

她逆黄河而上，翻越黑山。

She traveled upstream along the Yellow River, and traversed the Black Mountains.

她遇敌不惧，英勇作战。

She was very brave and fought gallantly, defeating many enemies.

木兰驰骋沙场十二年，屡建奇功。谁说女子不如男！

Mulan remained a warrior for twelve years, winning innumerable battles. Who says women are not as good as men!

图书在版编目 (CIP) 数据

中国经典故事. 1：英汉对照/熊亮主编；范晓星译.
北京：海豚出版社，2009.7
ISBN 978-7-80138-791-2

I. 中⋯ II.①熊⋯②范⋯ III.①英语－汉语－对照读
物②童话－作品集－中国 IV.H319.4：I

中国版本图书馆CIP数据核字（2009）第096436号

策　　　划：李富根
责任编辑：汪涛　王玮
封面设计：张媛媛

出　　　版：海豚出版社
出　版　人：李富根
网　　　址：http://www.dolphin-books.com.cn
地　　　址：北京市百万庄大街24号　　邮　　　编：100037
电　　　话：010-68997480（销售）　　　010-68326332（投稿）
传　　　真：010-68993503
印　　　刷：北京外文印刷厂
经　　　销：新华书店
开　　　本：24开（889毫米×1194毫米）
印　　　张：2
字　　　数：20千
版　　　次：2009年7月第1版　　　2009年7月第1次印刷
标准书号：ISBN 978-7-80138-791-2
定　　　价：14.00元